Listen to this St[ory]

Tales from the West In[dies]

When Grace Hallworth was a little girl in the West Indies, there was nothing she liked more than listening to and reading stories, especially the stories which were part of the islands' customs, folklore and humour. In her collection she has retold them with all the expressions of speech and vitality which she enjoyed so much: stories like *How Agouti Lost his Tail* and *How Crab Got its Back*, together with her own story version of how the Kiskadee bird got its name.

Also by Grace Hallworth

Mouth Open, Story Jump Out

for younger readers

Cric Crac

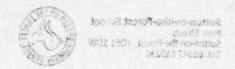

GRACE HALLWORTH

Listen to this Story
Tales from the West Indies

Illustrated by Dennis Ranston

MAMMOTH

This collection of stories
first published in Great Britain 1977
by Methuen Children's Books Ltd
Methuen paperback edition first published 1978
Magnet paperback edition first published 1985
Published 1992 by Mammoth
an imprint of Mandarin Paperbacks
Michelin House, 81 Fulham Road, London SW3 6RB

Mandarin is an imprint of the Octopus Publishing Group,
a division of Reed International Books Ltd

ISBN 0 7497 1058 6

A CIP catalogue record for this title
is available from the British Library

Printed in Great Britain
by Cox & Wyman Ltd, Reading, Berkshire

Contents

Introduction

When I was a little girl in Trinidad, an island in the West Indies, there was nothing I enjoyed more than listening to and reading stories.

One could read stories about giants and ogres, about dragons breathing fire and smoke, about princes who were put under spells and turned into frogs until a beautiful princess loved them, about genies who appeared when you rubbed old lamps, and all the enchantments of fairy-land.

But the stories which we children were told on a rainy day at school, when we could not go out to play, or when we sat at night on the porch with no other light but moonlight playing on our faces, and the trees around the house casting shapes and shadows so

7

frightening that we huddled close to each other as the storyteller wove magic with words—these stories were part of the land and the people of the West Indies. In them were the customs, the folklore, the expressions of speech and humour of the country, and if some of the animals in the stories were strange and unknown, well then that too was part of the magic.

Anancy, or ''Nanci stories' as they are sometimes called, might be about a meeting between the storyteller (or someone the story-teller knew) and one of the supernatural beings – 'lajablesse', 'soucouyan', 'douen' – very late one night; or it might be one of the Brer Anancy tales. It might even be a story woven round some person whom everyone knew or had heard about, like Gumbo Lie-Lie, who greased himself so well before he set out on his nightly prowls of mischief that no one could catch him. In fact, the term 'Nanci story is still used to describe something heard which is not believed.

In West Indian folklore, as in the folklore of many other countries, midnight is often a magic hour when anything can happen and dawn means danger for any supernatural beings still abroad. In the more traditional tales about Brer Anancy, or Bo Anancy as he is often called, he usually manages to triumph over bigger and stronger animals by using his wits; other stories set out to explain how and why things happened.

The West Indian folk tale comes from a people with a long tradition of oral storytelling. Stories are passed on by word of mouth by grandparents, by parents, by household servants and by children themselves. Each person has his or her own style, adds or omits parts of stories as he sees fit or as memory allows and so many versions of the same story abound.

In recent years some of these stories have been written down and published not only so that a wider audience might enjoy them, but also because this is one way of preserving the stories for West Indian children at home and abroad. In some of the stories in this collection, the manner of speech has been localized and the characters express themselves quite naturally in the way many of the storytellers would when telling the story. I have attempted to use these speech patterns or dialect where they add colour and humour to the story without making it too difficult for every-body to understand what is being said.

The Kiskadee is a story which I made up as a possible explanation of why the bird so called cries 'Qu'est-ce-qu'il dit?' from dawn till dusk, but all the other stories were told me by friends who remembered them, either in whole or in part, from their childhood.

I hope that you will listen to these 'Nanci stories and find enjoyment.

1 How Agouti lost his tail

Brer Anansi was often clever and Brer Anansi was often cunning, but Brer Anansi was something of a mischief-maker too.

There was a time when Brer Agouti and Brer Dog were very good friends and hunted in the forest together; but this is no longer true and it is all because of Brer Anansi.

One morning as Brer Agouti and Brer Dog hunted in the forest, Brer Anansi appeared puffing and panting, for he had come a long way and the sun was quite warm.

'How d'y do, compères?' he called to Dog and Agouti.

'Mornin', Brer Anansi. What are you doing up so early?' asked Brer Dog, for everyone knew that Brer Anansi never rose before noon unless he was up to mischief.

'Ah, compères, at daybreak I heard some news from Brer Cock that I cannot believe and neither will you when you hear it,' said Brer Anansi.

'What is it?' asked Brer Agouti anxiously. 'Is someone dead?'

'Well, you know how often we have sat around and talked about visiting Bird Island? Now I hear that Brer Cow is planning an excursion to Bird Island on Sunday and only animals with horns are invited!' said Brer Anansi.

'But we have no horns. Only Brer Bull, Brer Goat and Brer Ram will be able to go!' cried Brer Dog.

'What's to be done?' asked Brer Agouti. 'They are all bigger than we are, so it's no use getting angry with them.'

And the three of them talked and talked about what they could not do and they talked and talked about what they should not do. But no one could think of what they could do about it. Finally Brer Anansi departed to sew his seeds of mischief elsewhere.

But Dog and Agouti were very unhappy indeed, for it was one of their dearest wishes to visit Bird Island. They talked about it long after Anansi had gone and suddenly Brer Agouti had an idea.

They would find some wood and shape two pairs of horns, one for Dog and one for Agouti, and so disguised they would join the other animals on Sunday.

That week they searched the forests for smooth wood which they carefully shaped and polished until the horns shone bright in the sun. On Sunday morning early they arose and packed their picnic basket with roasted wild pig, breadfruit and sweet potatoes cooked in wood ash, and filled their flasks with pineapple juice laced with rum.

Then Dog said to Agouti, 'You fix my horns just above my ears and fix them well. Then I'll fix yours.'

And Agouti did so. Just as he had finished they heard the chant from the ship as the animals prepared to cast off:

'*Madinga oi Madinga*
Adokinde oi Madinga.'

'Hurry, hurry!' cried Agouti. 'You fix my horns now, Dog, or we shall be left behind.'

But Dog was not waiting for anyone; he was running as fast as he could and poor

Agouti was left behind. He could not join the animals now, for although he had made his horns he could not fix them to his head himself.

Agouti ran quickly to the hills behind the forest where there were three mountain peaks overlooking the harbour. As he came to the first peak the boat was just sailing by and he could see Dog standing on deck with all the other animals.

Agouti sang loud and clear:

> 'Captain oi, captain Cow!
> One of the animals has no horns!'

But Dog heard and ran to the captain and said, 'Did you hear that? He said, "Sail to the east, sail to the east!"'

And so the captain sailed on, bearing a bit to the east.

Agouti ran quickly to the second peak and as the boat sailed by he sang loud and clear:

> 'Captain oi, captain Cow!
> One of the animals has no horns!'

Again Dog heard and ran to the captain and said, 'Did you hear that? He said, "Sail to the west, sail to the west!"'

And so the captain sailed on, bearing a bit to the west.

Yet once more Agouti ran quickly, now to the third peak, and as the boat was sailing by he sang loud and clear:

> *'Captain oi, captain Cow!*
> *One of the animals has no horns!'*

This time the wind blew the words to the captain and he heard them loud and clear. He stopped the boat and, lining up all the animals, he began to test the horns of Brer Goat, Brer Ram, Brer Bull. . . . But before he could get to the end of the line, Brer Dog had leaped off the ship and was swimming for shore.

Mad with rage, he made for the mountain peak. But Agouti had seen him coming and was already running as fast as he could towards his hole.

Fast he ran but faster ran Dog who was just about to make the final leap when Agouti dived into his hole and 'Aa-aa-aa-aa-a-a-agh . . .' cried Agouti in pain, for Dog had got hold of his tail and bitten it off with his sharp teeth.

2 Compère Anansi and the pig

Compère Anansi's wife had a white pig which she had reared from a piglet. He had grown into a big, fat pig and she hoped to sell him at the market. But all the time Compère Anansi was thinking of a way to get that pig and eat it.

One day, as soon as he heard his wife returning from market, he climbed into bed, pulled the blanket over him and began to groan and rub his stomach.

'What troubles you my husband?' asked his wife.

'Aie! Aie!' groaned Compère Anansi, 'pain killin' me.'

His wife was very worried for he appeared to be very ill and she urged him to visit the doctor.

The very next day Compère Anansi got up early and left the house but he only pretended to visit the doctor. When he returned home he said to his wife, 'The doctor says that I must take a white pig up the hill, kill it and eat it all by myself, otherwise I may die.'

At these words Compère Anansi's wife became very angry. 'I rear that white pig from small,' she said, 'and now that it is big and ready for market you tell me I must kill it!'

'Well,' replied Compère Anansi in a huff, 'if you don't believe me, go and ask the doctor but go now or tomorrow may be too late!'

At once Compère Anansi's wife set out to visit the doctor.

Now Compère Anansi knew that every morning the doctor paid visits to people at home who were too ill to go to his surgery. So as soon as his wife was out of sight, Compère Anansi left the house, took a short cut by the forest track, and arrived at the doctor's surgery long before his wife got there.

Quickly he disguised himself and put on the doctor's long white coat. Then he sat behind the doctor's desk and waited. Some time later his wife arrived and thinking that Compère Anansi *was* the doctor, she told him all about the pig.

'Ahem! Aha! I see your problem', said Compère Anansi, trying to sound as clever as the doctor. 'But if your husband does *not* eat the white pig, he may die.'

Compère Anansi's wife wept and she pleaded, but at last she agreed to give Anansi the pig. When she returned home there was Compère Anansi in bed, tossing and groaning as though he was in a fever.

'Aie! Aie! I'm sure to die,' he moaned. And indeed he looked so ill that his wife went quickly to the pig pen and brought the pig for Anansi. Before you could say, 'crick! crack!' Compère Anansi was out of bed, leading the pig up the hill.

He lit a wood fire and put on a large pan filled with water and some herbs. While he was waiting for the water to boil, he decided to go down to the river to catch some crayfish to add flavour to the pig stew.

Once, Compère Anansi put his hand in the river and caught nothing. Twice, he put his hand in the river and caught nothing. But the

19

third time something caught hold of his hand and started to pull him in.

Compère Anansi tried to free himself, but could not. He pulled and pulled – and suddenly, up came Mapapire, the river snake, holding fast to Anansi's hand.

'Compère Anansi', said Mapapire, 'if you give me some of what you cookin' up there on the hill, I'll let you go.'

'But I ain't have nuthin' cookin', Mapapire,' replied Compère Anansi. 'That smoke you see up there is from some trees the woodcutter is burning on the hill.'

'Compère Anansi,' said Mapapire, 'I watch you all morning, so I *know* you cookin' something. Take me up there if you want to live.'

Well in the end, Compère Anansi *had* to give in, and the two of them went up the hill.

When Mapapire saw the fat, white pig tied up to a tree, and smelt the herbs in the boiling water, he flicked his tongue greedily and said, 'Compère Anansi, let me soften the pig for you. He will cook quicker and we will enjoy him sooner.'

Compère Anansi did not trust Mapapire

but the snake was bigger and stronger than Anansi so he agreed.

Mapapire swallowed the pig in one gulp.

Now Compère Anansi was really angry; he was so angry that he called to Compère Corbeau who was flying overhead, and told him to seize Mapapire and take him high up in the sky. So Corbeau swooped down and took Mapapire in his big, strong claws.

'How high up shall I take him?' asked Compère Corbeau.

'High, high up' called Compère Anansi.

Compère Corbeau flew a bit higher and then he called out again to Anansi, 'How much higher?'

'Much, much higher,' shouted Compère Anansi.

Compère Corbeau was now flying so high in the sky, that he could no longer hear Anansi. Besides, Mapapire was getting heavier and heavier, so at last Corbeau had to drop him.

Down, down, down dropped Mapapire. The wind blew him this way and that way and at last he dropped plop, squash, right in the pig pen where Compère Anansi's wife was sitting crying over the loss of her pig.

Imagine her surprise when she saw her fat, white pig wriggling his way out of the belly of the dead snake.

He was quite unhurt and as fit for market as ever, and that is just where Compère Anansi's wife took her pig straight away.

3 How trouble made
the monkey eat pepper

An old woman used to buy molasses from a
nearby village. One day as she was returning
home she tripped over the roots of a tree and
her calabash fell and broke, spilling the
molasses she had just bought.

When the old woman saw her molasses
running on the ground and going to waste she
began to cry:

> *'Lordie, Lordie, look at mi trouble, oui,*
> *Lordie, Lordie, how trouble overtake me!'*

She scooped up as much of the molasses as
she could with a bit of broken calabash and
continued on her way. As soon as she had
gone, Monkey climbed down from the tree
where he had seen and heard all that had happened.

23

He sniffed the treacly, sweet syrup on the ground and in no time he had licked it all up.

'Yum, yum!' he said, smacking his lips, 'if this is trouble then I'll have double.' And off he ran to the village shop to buy some trouble.

Now when Monkey entered the shop and asked for double trouble, the shopkeeper could make neither head nor tail of it. So Monkey explained what had happened to the old woman. Then the shopkeeper saw his chance of getting even with Monkey, who had pelted him with coconuts the last time he had taken a short cut through the forest.

He went to the back of the shop, seized two bull-dogs sleeping there and put them into a sack which he tied securely. Then he returned to the shop and handed the sack to Monkey.

'There's enough trouble in here to keep you busy for quite a while,' said the shopkeeper.

Without so much as an 'If you please,' or a 'Thank you,' Monkey threw the money down on the counter, grabbed the sack and rushed off. He ran deep, deep into the forest until he came to a quiet shady patch under a gru-gru palm where he sat down and made ready to enjoy trouble. No sooner had he opened the sack than the two bull-dogs jumped out and rushed to attack him. Monkey barely had time to leap to a branch of the gru-gru palm and there he crouched, not daring to move, the hot sun burning into his skin and the thorns digging into his paws and the bull-dogs baying and barking at the foot of the tree.

Thus it was that the shopkeeper found Monkey late, late that evening when he went to look for his dogs.

'Ah Monkey! What trouble is this I see?
Double trouble wait under this tree!'

said the shopkeeper.

Poor Monkey was so faint and weak he could hardly speak. Growing quite near was a pepper tree laden with red-hot peppers. He had eaten nothing all day and peppers, even red-hot peppers, were better than nothing. Monkey reached out and devoured pepper after pepper until there wasn't a pepper left on the tree.

Tears ran down his face and as the pepper burned his tongue, his mouth and his stomach, Monkey gasped:

'I have had my fill of trouble,
Hungry and thirsty I'm seeing double.'

'Then' said the shopkeeper, 'take my advice, Monkey, and never trouble trouble unless trouble trouble you.'

4 How crab got its back

In a village there once lived two sisters who were as different from each other as chalk from cheese.

Esmeralda, the younger sister, was plain as plain could be, but she was kind to everyone and worked from morning till night scrubbing and cleaning their little house so that it was as neat as a pin. Yolanda, the elder sister, was the most beautiful girl in the village, but she was proud and haughty and never a finger would she lift to help her sister.

One day Esmeralda went to the river to fill her goblet and she saw, sitting at the water's edge, a strange old woman. Around the woman's waist was wrapped a towel, but her back was bare and she was trying to scoop up

27

water in her thin, wasted hands to wash her back.

When she saw Esmeralda she began to sing in a voice that was high and shrill:

> *'Scratch my back, daughter, oh!*
> *Wash it well with water, oh!'*

Esmeralda saw that the old woman's back was lined and very sore and she felt very sorry for her, and although the old woman's back felt as hard as board, Esmeralda scratched it and washed it until her nails were broken. But as soon as she stopped the old woman began to complain and to sing:

> *'Scratch my back, daughter, oh!*
> *Wash it well with water, oh!'*

And although the old woman's back felt as sharp as broken bottles, Esmeralda scratched it and washed it until her hands were bleeding.

Then the old woman said in a voice as gentle as a pigeon's cooing, 'Child, you have been patient and kind to a miserable old woman and I should like to give you something in return. What do you wish for most?'

Esmeralda felt ashamed to ask anything of

28

one who seemed so much in need, so she replied, 'Just your blessing, mother.'

'Well,' said the old woman, 'you may have that and more. Look in the water, Esmeralda, and you shall see what you will be!'

Imagine Esmeralda's surprise when she looked in the water and saw not her plain face but the most beautiful, the kindest face she had ever seen. She raised her head to thank the old woman but the old woman had vanished.

At first Yolanda could not believe that this beautiful girl was indeed Esmeralda whom she had scorned and ill-treated all her life. She was green with envy, and without waiting to hear the whole story she rushed down to the river, for she thought, 'Stupid Esmeralda! Where does she think a pretty face will get her? I shall ask for great wealth. Then I shan't have to share that pigs' pen with her!'

As Yolanda went down to the river she saw, sitting at the water's edge, the ugliest old woman she had ever set eyes on. Her hands and feet were shrivelled until they looked like claws, and her bare back was crossed by so many lines that it looked as though it were cracked all over. When the old woman saw

Yolanda she began to sing in a voice that was high and shrill:

> *'Scratch my back, daughter, oh!*
> *Wash it well with water, oh!'*

But Yolanda was in a fever of impatience to find the source of her sister's good fortune.

Nor did she know that she had found it, for she had only one wicked thought in her head.

'Out of my way, you ugly creature!' she cried. 'Do you expect me to wallow in the mud with you! Scratch your back with those claws of yours!' And she pushed the old woman to one side.

'Insolent girl!' said the old woman. 'As you see *me* so shall *you* be!'

And at that moment Yolanda became an ugly creature, her limbs shrivelled up and turned into her claws and her back became hard and cracked all over.

She cannot now bear to be seen, for she remembers that once she was beautiful. So she wallows in the mud and hides away under rocks and cliffs. And when sand and mud fill the cracks and her back itches, she rushes down to the river to wash it off for no one will scratch her back.

5 Compère Anansi and the Cows

There was once a widow who owned a piece of land on which nothing grew but zootie grass. She wanted to clear the land to grow crops, but she could get no one to clear it for her. For you must know that if zootie grass touches the skin it itches and burns like fire.

The grass grew so high, that not even the cattle would graze in the field. So eventually the widow announced that she would give a big, red cow to anyone who could clear the grass, without *once* scratching until the task was finished.

When the villagers heard the news, they flocked to the widow's house to try their luck, for a cow was like a pot of gold to them.

In to the field they went, one after the

other, and out of the field they came, one after the other. The zootie grass got on their hands and faces; it got inside their shoes and down their backs, and they would start to scratch and scratch, until they could bear it no longer.

One day, Compère Anansi was passing through the village and heard about the widow's offer. He decided there and then to win the cow. By the time he got there, a third of the field had been cleared already.

He had only cleared a small patch of grass, when his skin began to itch and burn. He stood it for as long as he could, but just as he was about to scratch, he looked up and saw the widow's son spying on him through some bushes.

Compère Anansi began to puff and pant, then he called to the boy in a hoarse voice, 'Boy, boy, I must have some water before I die of thirst. Run quick and fetch some water from the river, in this cocoa basket.'

The boy was so surprised at the request, that he ran off at once to fetch the water. But the cocoa basket was full of holes, and no matter how hard the boy tried he could not fill it. By the time the boy returned Compère Anansi's scratching was over.

After a while, Compère Anansi had a strong urge to scratch again. So he said, 'Boy, boy, let me give you a dasheen to fill the holes in the basket. But jump high or jump low, I must have water.' So he gave the boy a dasheen and sent him to the river again.

The little boy tried to fill the holes in the basket with the dasheen, but every time he put the basket in the water, the dasheen fell out. By the time he returned, Compère

35

Anansi had scratched to his heart's content and was working away again.

When Compère Anansi had almost finished clearing the grass, he began to itch all over his body. He looked across the field and saw the big, red cow grazing. So he called out, 'Boy, boy, uo' see that cow grazing? He red by here and he red by there. He red down here and he red up there. He red ...' And Compère Anansi continued talking, and scratching each part of his body as he pointed to it, until the terrible itch was soothed.

At last, all the grass was cleared and Compère Anansi won the big, red cow.

But Compère Anansi was not happy. True, he had a big, red cow but Compère Tigre had *two* red cows, and that made him the most important man in the village.

Everyday, Compère Anansi looked over his fence and saw two cows in his neighbour's backyard. And if looks could kill, those two cows would have dropped down dead long ago.

But Compère Anansi was a patient man, and he could await his chance.

One night, as he was walking home through the forest, he saw a dead, wild hog lying right in the middle of the track. It had been dead for several days and the vultures had picked it clean. But the head and legs were still in one piece.

As Compère Anansi looked at the carcase in front of him, he suddenly had an idea. 'Aha!' he said to himself, 'everything comes to him who waits!' And he set about cutting off the legs and the head of the wild hog. Then he put them in his sack and took them home.

All next day he stayed at home, shaping a bit of sacking to look like the body of a cow, and filling it with a bit of this and a bit of that. Then he sewed it up, all except four little holes

37

for the hog's feet and one big hole for the head.

Now Compère Tigre used to take his produce to market every Friday morning and return home just after sunset. So on Friday, just as it got dark, Compère Anansi took the stuffed animal to the path which led to Compère Tigre's house. He placed the animal on its back in the ditch and covered it with mud and stones. But he left the legs sticking up so that they could be seen from the path. Then he went back into his house and waited for Compère Tigre's return.

A few minutes later, he heard footsteps and then Compère Tigre called out, 'Compère Anansi, yo' cow fall in the ditch.'

'Pull it up Compère,' cried Anansi, 'pull it up for me, but be careful how yo' pull, because if yo' pull off the feet, yo' have to pay me for the cow.'

Compère Tigre rushed back to pull up the cow. He was not worried about Compère Anansi's threat, for whoever heard of a cow's legs coming off!

Compère Anansi followed behind, but not too fast, not too fast. Then Compère Tigre pulled the cow by the feet. But to his surprise, he fell back on to the path with all four hog's legs in his hands.

And Compère Anansi? Well, he bought another cow with the money Compère Tigre paid him.

6 The Kiskadee

For three months and three weeks there had been no rain.

El Tucuche, the oldest range of mountains, was angry with Rain Cloud. His jagged peaks were dry and burned, his ridges were swept bare by winds and storms, and there were deep furrows in his sides caused by fires from the heat of the sun.

'I protect the forests from the heat of the sun and the fury of the sea winds,' said he, 'yet every morning Rain Cloud showers the forests of my brothers and keeps them green and fresh and though I have begged her these many years for some of the precious water she gives me none.'

For although El Tucuche was the oldest mountain, he was not the tallest. Behind him

41

were his two brothers, El Cerro, the tallest, and El Blanco, the youngest of the three. When Rain Cloud came in from the sea filled with water, she sailed over El Tucuche with ease, but El Cerro's tall peaks forced her to rise, and spill the precious water which showered down on to the forests below.

And so El Tucuche raged and fumed, and when Rain Cloud tried to cross over, El Tucuche stretched up tall, tall, taller than El Cerro, and would not let her in.

So no rain now reached the forests below El Cerro.

The gushing mountain streams became mere trickles of water, the deep cool ponds where the crapaud and frogs used to live were nothing but muddy swamps, and even the great rivers were nearly empty and would soon be dry beds, baked hard in the sun.

El Tigre, the tiger, called a meeting of all the animals in the forest. They met at daybreak when it was cool in the forest. This was the time of day when Fly-catcher Bird made her morning rounds to drink the fresh dew and to feed on her diet of insects before Sun climbed over the mountain and forced the flowers open to rob them of the refreshing drink.

As Fly-catcher flitted from flower to flower she heard the sound of voices. In a clearing in the forest the animals were discussing their plight.

El Tigre said, 'For three months and three weeks there has been no rain. We must find Rain-spirit soon, otherwise our children will be killed by the drought.'

Ti Manicou said, 'But where shall we find him? No one knows where he hides during the day.'

Batit Mamselle said, 'Perhaps Owl can help us. She doesn't say much, but she sees and hears a great deal.'

And so after a long palaver it was decided that Bo Corbeau should visit Owl that night.

Now Fly-catcher was a most inquisitive creature and a great gossip into the bargain. She often caused trouble among the animals by repeating what she thought she heard and not what was said, so no one had bothered to invite her to the meeting. Hidden between the thick branches of a cedar tree she strained to hear. But she was too high up and could only hear a few words here and there.

When the meeting broke up Fly-catcher flew off to find Rain-spirit. She knew where he lived, for on her early morning rounds she often saw the little green spirit dancing and leaping through the forest as his gentle showers washed the earth, the trees, and the flowers, after their night's sleep. And she had followed him to his home one day.

In a dark silent part known as the Rain Forest, where the trees were always clothed with leaves of deepest green, where moss and fungus covered the bark of the trees, and the grass sparkled with silver raindrops, the small spirit sat on a tree stump. He looked tired and sad.

'Bonjour, mon ami,' greeted Fly-catcher. 'Comment ça va?' (In those days the animals spoke *patois* which is not very good French, but Fly-catcher boasted that she always spoke the very best French.)

'Comme çi, comme ça,' replied Rain-spirit sadly, and before he could tell Fly-catcher his troubles she began to relate all that had taken place that morning. She begged him to leave the island before the animals found him and killed him, as she assured him they planned to do.

Rain-spirit was angry when he heard all this for he had returned that very morning from a week of pleading with El Tucuche to let Rain Cloud in. When that had failed he had spent three sleepless nights trying to find a way to get Rain Cloud in with the precious water. Slowly a plan had taken shape in his mind; he would make another and larger Rain Cloud and while one showered El Tucuche the other would sail on to the forests beyond. But when he heard what Fly-catcher said, he stamped his foot and spun around three times chanting as he spun:

> *'Rain, rain go to New Spain*
> *And never, never return again.'*

Then he rose into the air and flew away, away over the trees, the mountains, the sea, until he was a small speck in the sky.

As the weeks passed things went from bad to worse. The leaves began to fall from the trees and the animals found little shade from the sun; the earth was dry and parched and the grass began to wither; flowers faded and drooped on their limp stalks, and birds and insects sought in vain for dew and honey; the streams and rivers dried up and the animals wandered far and wide in their search for water.

46

Bo Corbeau looked everywhere, but could find no trace of Rain-spirit. One morning he set out earlier than usual and met Fly-catcher. She had not fared as badly as the other animals, for she had found a little pool of fresh water in the Rain Forest and flew there every morning to drink her fill.

Bo Corbeau noticed how well Fly-catcher looked. He noticed too that her feathers were shining and moist. But he merely greeted her and pretended to fly away. As soon as she thought that she was alone she headed for the Rain Forest. Bo Corbeau kept a safe distance so that she should not see him. He saw her alight and hop to a small pool of water. Before she could take her first sip, he swooped down and stood facing her. 'You miserable, selfish creature!' he said angrily. 'So this is how you live while everyone else goes without water. I shall take you to El Tigre and the animals shall sit in council over you this very night.'

But Fly-catcher was clever and knew that only one thing could save her. The most important law of the forest was that no animal or creature should take or use that which belonged to another without consent. Without this law there could be no peace or justice

47

in the forest. So when Fly-catcher was brought before the council meeting she said, 'The pool belongs to the Rain-spirit who gave me leave before he left to take whatever I needed. But according to the law of the forest I could not offer to anyone else what was not mine to offer.'

'And I suppose you know where Rain-spirit is?' enquired El Tigre.

'Mais oui!' replied Fly-catcher. 'I overheard your wicked plan to kill him and I warned him. Now he has left the island and gone to New Spain.'

In the excitement that followed this news Fly-catcher was forgotten and quickly flew away. Bo Corbeau was sent post-haste to New Spain (which is now called South America) to seek out Rain-spirit and explain what had happened.

After searching for three days Bo Corbeau found Rain-spirit, who was only too pleased to return, for he was lonely in the dense, strange jungle and missed his own Rain Forest very much. When he returned he made his second Rain-cloud and his plan was a great success.

Now El Tucuche is no longer burned and

dry. His ridges and peaks are covered with trees which are as green and as beautiful as those in the forest. All through the year the valleys are ablaze with the colourful blossoms of the yellow poui, the pink poui, the immortelle, which shades the cocoa plants, the cassia, the frangipani and the beautiful queen of flowers.

From dawn to dusk a bird flits in and out of the trees calling sadly, 'Qu-est-ce-qu'il dit? Qu-est-ce-qu'il dit?' It is Fly-catcher and she asks everyone she meets, 'What is he saying? What is he saying?' For the animals decided to punish Fly-catcher for the suffering she had caused them, by changing their language. What they speak, neither you, nor I, nor Fly-catcher can understand, so she can never again repeat what she hears. She can only ask, 'Qu'est-ce-qu'il dit? Qu'est-ce-qu'il dit?' And everyone mocks her and calls her Kiskadee.

7 The courting of Miss Annie

Brer Anansi and Brer Tiger were both in love with Miss Annie and went callin' every night. Sometimes Miss Annie favoured Anansi, other times she favoured Tiger, but she could not decide which of them to marry. All the time Anansi was scheming and conniving and thinking of a way to win Miss Annie's favour.

One night Brer Anansi invited the minstrels—Bo Bull, Compère Cricket, Brer Donkey and Ti Humming Bird—to his house. He plied them with pigeon peas, bananas and cane juice with mollasses, then he dropped some remarks about Brer Tiger in a casual way.

A few days later everyone was singing a

song and sniggering as they sang, and this
was what they sang:

> *Tiger walk, Tiger talk,*
> *Tiger eatin' with knife and fork,*
> *Jingo lay-oh, Anansi ride him all day.*
> *Tiger boasts, Tiger roars, but*
> *Tiger creepin' round on all fours.*
> *Jingo-lay-oh, Anansi ride him all day.'*

And so the next time Tiger went calling on
Miss Annie, she gave him the rough edge of
her tongue. 'Tiger, you have a nerve to come
here talkin' 'bout marriage. You are nuthin'
but a low-born jackass and Anansi's jackass at
that.'

'It ain't true,' Tiger pleaded. 'It ain't true,'
Tiger swore.

Miss Annie's pride was hurt; he was shown
the door.

'All right, I'm going,' said Tiger. 'But you
wait and see. When I return with Anansi,
what will your tune be?'

And he rushed away into the forest roaring
angrily, so that all the animals gathered at
Miss Annie's to ask why and wherefore.

In the forest Anansi too heard Tiger's roars
and knowing what he knew he ran to his

house and locked the door. No sooner had he done so than he heard Tiger roar just outside the door. With one blow Tiger broke the door down and strode in.

'So I'm *your* jackass, Anansi,' said Tiger. 'Well, I'm carrying you back and if you repeat what you said to the others, you'll be *my* meat.'

He threw Anansi across his shoulder and started back to Miss Annie. By and by Tiger came to a stream which was swollen from the rains. The water was up to his knees and was slowly rising.

Anansi began to slip and to slide off Tiger's back. 'Too weak, Brer Tiger. Too weak to stay on. If I get wet with this fever I'll be a dead man,' said he in a very faint voice.

Overhanging the stream were the vines of some liane trees which grew on the bank. Tiger cut a piece of the vine and gave it to Anansi. He took off his coat and said, 'Put the vine around my neck and hold on to it, and throw the coat over you to keep you warm. But weak or not, Anansi, I'm carrying you back, and if you repeat what you said to the others, you'll be *my* meat.'

Anansi did as he was bid and soon they

53

were on their way. Suddenly Tiger came to a halt, coughing and spluttering. 'Anansi, you tryin' to choke me with the vine or what?' he asked angrily.

'Too fast, Brer Tiger! I'm all out of breath. Why take me back if I'm silent in death?' gasped Anansi.

Lying on the ground were some dried branches blown down by the storm. Tiger picked one up and gave it to Anansi. 'Take this branch and when I go too fast, nudge me with it. But out of breath or not, Anansi, I'm carrying you back, and if you repeat what you said to the others, you'll be *my* meat.'

They had gone some distance when they saw Miss Annie's cat stalking a bird. Anansi began to moan and to groan. 'A-i-ee, a-i-ee. I mus' die if I mus'. Best kill me now Brer Tiger, or fetch little puss.'

'Why should I fetch little puss?' asked Tiger. 'After all, I carried you this distance without any help and we've only a little way to go.'

'Ah, Brer Tiger,' replied Anansi, and his voice was just a whisper, 'you brave and you strong, but this time you wrong. For though

54

puss is small she can walk on all fours. I can't go an inch further this way.'

So Tiger, who had always walked upright, went down on all fours. With Tiger's coat Anansi made a saddle to sit on. He held fast to the vine around Tiger's neck, and in his hand was the dead branch. Tiger went slowly, for he was not used to walking this way, and in this manner they approached Miss Annie's house.

When Brer Anansi saw Miss Annie and all

the animals gathered on the verandah, he tugged at the vine, whipped Brer Tiger with the branch and shouted, 'Gidyap! Gidyap!'

As they rode past Miss Annie he shouted, 'See what I tell you, Miss Annie. Brer Tiger's nuthin' but a jackass and I ridin' him all the way!'

Miss Annie and the animals clapped and laughed and cheered Anansí, but Tiger was going as fast as wind and roaring as he went at the shame of it.

Tiger still goes on four legs, and as for Miss Annie, she never married anyone.

'Jingo lay-oh, Anansi ride him all day!'

8 Quaka Raja

There was once a poor widow who lived in a hut at the edge of the forest with her four children.

She favoured her three daughters – Minnie Minnie, Minnie Bitana, and Philambo – but she did not care a wit for her son, Quaka Raja, Yet Quaka Raja was obedient and worked hard in the vegetable garden in front of the hut while his three sisters quarrelled and fought among themselves all day. They made fun of Quaka because he was kind to the birds and animals of the forest, and always saved some of his food for them.

Every Friday the widow set out for the village market where she sold the vegetables and fruit from her garden. Everyone flocked to buy her dasheen, yams, sweet potatoes, mangoes, sapodillas, peas and beans, and soon her basket was empty. With the money she received she bought food to take home and filled her basket with all manner of goodies. There was Arape, a cornmeal pancake with spicy meat filling, molasses balls, sugar cakes, black pudding, and many other things besides.

When she returned to the little hut she stood outside and sang:

> *'Minnie Minnie, come here,*
> *Minnie Bitana, come here,*
> *Philambo, come here,*
> *Leave Quaka Raja one dey.'*

As soon as the three daughters heard the song they ran to unlock the door, pushing Quaka Raja aside as the mother did not want him. Then the food was shared. But Quaka Raja's portion was always the least of all.

Now in the forest lived a man called Zobolak who was feared by all the villagers. He was a hideous-looking creature, with a deeply scarred face, fiery red eyes, and arms and legs that were huge and round, with clawlike hands and feet. Mothers warned their children to keep away from the forest, for whenever a child disappeared it was whispered that Zobolak had stolen it, though no one could prove this was true.

One Friday, when the widow returned from market, Zobolak, who had been hunting agouti, happened to be nearby. Peeping through the bushes he heard the widow's song and saw the three daughters run out to greet their mother. Zobolak could hardly restrain himself from rushing forward and seizing the three girls then and there, but he was as cunning as the wild animals which he hunted in the forest. He settled down to wait.

The next Friday the widow again set out for market. After some time had passed, Zobolak crept up to the hut and sang in a high voice:

> *'Minnie Minnie, come here,*
> *Minnie Minnie, come here,*
> *Minnie Minnie, come here,*
> *Leave Quaka Raja one dey.'*

The three daughters ran to open the door, but Quaka Raja said, 'Sisters, sisters, do not go out. That is not Mamma's song.' And he stood in front of the door and would not let them out even though they tugged and pulled until they were exhausted.

When the children did not open the door, Zobolak hid in the forest until the mother returned. But he stayed close by to listen carefully to the song.

The following Friday the mother set off once more for the village, and after a little while Zobolak crept up to the hut and sang in a high voice:

> *'Minnie Minnie, come here,*
> *Minnie Minnie, come here,*
> *Philambo, come here,*
> *Leave Quaka Raja one dey.'*

The three daughters ran to unlock the door, but Quaka Raja said, 'Sisters, sisters, do not go out. That is not Mamma's song.'

They tugged and pulled and scratched him but he stood fast in front of the door, and at last they fell down exhausted.

Once more Zobolak crept away into the forest when they did not open the door, but he waited close by until the mother returned.

At last Friday came. Zobolak's eyes gleamed with excitement as he waited. No sooner had the widow left than he crept up to the hut and sang in a high voice:

> *'Minnie, Minnie, come here,*
> *Minnie Bitana, come here,*
> *Philambo, come here,*
> *Leave Quaka Raja one dey.'*

Quaka Raja stood in front of the door and begged his sisters not to go out. Their mother had just left. How could she be back so soon? But they tugged and pulled and scratched and kicked him so hard that he fell to the ground, senseless.

They ran out to greet their mother, but – 'Ayayayayay!' – there was Zobolak waiting for them. He threw them into his sack, slung it over his shoulder and off he went into the forest where he lived.

By the time Quaka Raja came to his senses Zobolak was far, far away. Quaka Raja ran hither and yon calling his sisters, but only the birds cheeped back at him. When his mother returned from the village and he told her what had happened, she was wild with grief. But Quaka Raja said, 'Do not cry, Mamma, I will go and look for my sisters and bring them back to you.'

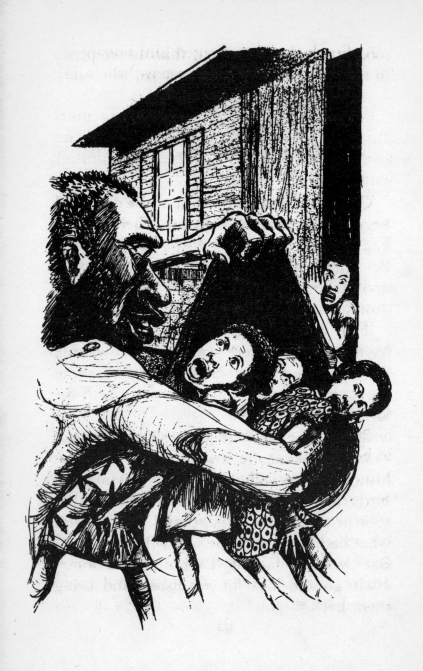

At first his mother begged him not to go. 'Son, you are all that I have now,' she said; 'I cannot lose you too.'

But Quaka Raja pleaded with her until she agreed. So she packed him some of the food she had brought back and sent him off with tears in her eyes.

Quaka walked long and he walked far. He walked all day, and as night fell he saw a light in the distance. As he approached it he came to a hut half hidden by trees and creepers. Inside he could hear his sisters crying.

What to do? He could not rescue them without help. As he stood under a tree thinking, an owl overhead hooted and nearly frightened him out of his wits. At that moment he thought of a plan. He could ask his friends, the birds and animals of the forest, to help him.

Much later that night, as the moon climbed down behind the mountain, the stillness of the forest was shattered by a horrible noise. Zobolak was startled out of his sleep as the sound grew louder and louder and came nearer and nearer, like the shrieks of a hundred demons coming after him. He rushed out of his hut

63

like a hunted animal and ran deep into the forest, over the mountains, anywhere away from that terrible noise.

What was that noise? It was the sound of owls hooting, frogs croaking, wild cats yowling, wild pigs snorting and grunting, parrots screaming and birds chirping and whistling. They had all come to help Quaka Raja.

So Quaka Raja returned home with his sisters and his mother was so proud of him that if he weren't such a sensible child he would have been thoroughly spoiled.

And for all we know Zobolak is still running!

9 Brer Anansi and Brer Snake

Time and again Brer Anansi would get into trouble because of his boasting. Most times he was clever enough to outsmart the other animals, then he would be quiet for a while. But it was no use: sooner or later he would join a group of animals talking, mouth would open and tongue would run away with him.

One day he heard Brer Dog saying to Brer Agouti, 'Boy, Brer Snake really swift. I see him whip himself round Brer Crocodile and squeeze the life out of him before you could say....'

Up piped Anansi: 'Ah, but that was only because Crocodile not used to land. Now if that was *me*, Brer Snake could never catch me.'

Another time he interrupted a discussion

between Brer Bull and Brer Ram. Brer Bull was modestly agreeing that Brer Snake was very strong indeed, stronger even than Brer Bull.

'Ah,' said Anansi, 'Brer Snake have brute strength but when it come to a real test of endurance I could beat him every time.'

The animals were getting a bit tired of Anansi's boasts, so it was not surprising that rumours reached Brer Snake that Anansi was bad talkin' him all over the forest.

Early one morning Brer Snake set out for Anansi's house. *Swish! Swish!* He was going to thrash Anansi so soundly that he would be too ashamed to show his face in the forest for many a month.

'Brer Anansi,' hissed Snake very loud, 'you sayin' all over the forest that you're a better man than me. Come out and prove it.'

Inside his house Brer Anansi trembled when he heard Snake's voice.

'Mornin', Brer Snake,' called Anansi. 'I sayin' my prayers but I will come out as soon as I ready.'

He knew that he could not escape, for peeping out he could see Brer Snake stretched full-length outside the only door. Anansi sat down on his bed and racked his brain. 'Ah ha!' he thought:

'Snake swift and he strong,
Snake soft and he long,
But today we go prove who right and who wrong.'

Quickly Anansi took all his belts and began to sew them together until he made one broad belt which covered his body from shoulder to legs.

Again Snake called out, 'Anansi, you takin' too long to say your prayers. Don't make me come in and get you or it will be worse for you.'

'Have patience, Brer Snake,' pleaded Anansi. 'I puttin' on my clothes. I will come out as soon as I ready.'

Hastily he began to hook some knives on to the belt so that the belt was like an armour. The knives were razor sharp.

This time Snake's voice was full of venom. 'Anansi, all your friends waitin' out here to see what a strong man you are, so if you don't come out I comin' in for you.' And indeed all the animals of the forest had gathered outside Anansi's door to see Snake punish Anansi.

Poor Anansi. His hands shook as he struggled to button his coat over the belt full of knives and his voice trembled as he called out, 'Have pity, Brer Snake. At least let me die with my boots on. I puttin' on my boots and then I will be ready.'

At last Anansi went out. There was Snake, his tail swishing angrily. He was ready to thrash this upstart.

Some of the animals were taking bets that Anansi would be down for the count of three,

others that he would be down at the first flick. The cautious ones were placing bets for two flicks.

Then once, twice, Snake swished his tail, and – *flick! flick!* – as it struck Anansi's coat Snake suddenly let out a *hisssssssss* of pain. His whole body began to writhe and turn and he hissed and hissed as the blood poured from the deep cuts on his tail.

Slowly and painfully he dragged himself through the forest to his hole, there to hide until his wounds were healed and his proud boasts were forgotten.

But Anansi knew that Snake would not rest until he had got even with him, so he too fled into the forest and found a place to hide. And this time he made sure that there was more than one door.

10 Fresh Fish

Compère Anansi had a longing for fried fish. Every day, as he passed by the river, he saw the fish swimming under the clear water, but he was too lazy to go fishing by himself.

One day, he met Compère Tigre and Mosha Flea, the Candlefly, and he invited them to go fishing with him that night. Compère Anansi told each of them what his job would be. Mosha Flea would give as much light as he could; Compère Tigre would catch the fish and Compère Anansi would sort the fish into piles for each of them.

All night they fished, and by day-break there was a large catch of fish on the river bank. Now it was time for Compère Anansi to share out the fish, so he began to count:

'One for me, one for Flea, one for Tigre and one for His.'

Compère Tigre and Mosha Flea looked at one another, then at Compère Anansi for an explanation. But Compère Anansi continued to count, as he placed the fish in little heaps.

At last Compère Tigre could stand it no longer and asked Anansi, 'But who is *His*?'

'How yo' mean, who is His?' exclaimed Anansi. 'Yo' must know who is His!'

Compère Tigre did not want to seem foolish, so he said nothing more, but he

72

watched the heap for His growing bigger and bigger.

When all the fish was shared out, Mosha Flea piped up in his small voice, 'Compère Anansi, only three of us fish here tonight, yet you have a share for a fourth. So who is *His*?'

'Look man, I don't have to answer foolish questions,' shouted Anansi. 'If you and Tigre don't like the way I share, I could throw all the fish back in the river.'

Poor Compère Tigre and Mosha Flea did not want to lose their share, so they gathered their heaps of fish and left, while Compère Anansi went off with twice as many fish as Tigre and Flea had received.

Compère Anansi had to pass Compère Lion's house on his way home. Now he always tested the ground hereabouts, as Compère Lion set traps on his land to catch other animals.

Compère Anansi threw some large stones to see if the ground was firm. Unfortunately, one of the stones fell on the house and woke up Compère Lion and his wife. Quietly they crept up behind Compère Anansi. What luck! They had caught Compère Anansi *and* a basketful of fresh fish into the bargain. Here was enough food to last them for a week or two.

They put Compère Anansi into a cage, and Compère Lion's wife hurried off to buy some fat for frying, while Compère Lion went to see if any animals had been caught in his traps.

When Lion's three children woke up and saw Anansi in the cage, and the basket full of lovely fish, they made up a tune on heir banjo and danced around the cage singing:

'Nansi bring us fish so sweet
Nansi bring us food to eat
Nansi will provide the meat
'Cos afterwards we go him eat.'

'Ay, ay, but all yo' can play the banjo nice, man,' said Anansi. 'I can play too, you know. Lend me yo' banjo and I'll show you.'

The foolish children opened the cage door to give Anansi the banjo, and before you could say 'Lion' he was out. He siezed them and cut out their tongues, just like that. But before he could escape, he heard Compère Lion and his wife entering the house. Quick

74

as a flash, Anansi climbed up into the attic and began to play the banjo and sing loudly:

> *'A hundred lions to fight, me-one*
> *I cut off their tongues.*
> *A hundred lions to fight, me-one*
> *I pull out their tails*
> *A hundred lions to fight me-one . . .'*

When Compère Lion and his wife saw what Anansi had done to their children and heard his threats, they took off at great speed through the forest with the children following as best they could. They never once stopped to look behind them until they had put many, many miles between them and Compère Anansi.

Even to his day, some people say if you want to scare off a lion, just shout, 'fresh fish!'

Some West Indian words

A wild animal rather like a hare which lives in the forest.

Agouti

Similar to a Jamaican patty, except that the outer case is made with cornmeal instead of pastry.

Arape
(*pron.* a-rape)

Similar in appearance to its English counterpart, but it has a spicier filling.

Black pudding

Breadfruit 	A round starchy fruit about the size of a football. It has a tough green skin and a corky centre; eaten as a vegetable.
Cassava	Starchy roots of a large shrub; eaten as a vegetable.
Corbeau	A vulture which is entirely black and can be found around refuse tips, abbatoirs and sandy beaches where they eat the fish thrown away by fishermen.
Dasheen	Starchy roots of a herb plant; eaten as a vegetable.
Frangipani tree	Tree which produces very sweet-smelling blossom; stem has a milky juice which stains.
Gru-gru palm	A prickly palm tree with small green fruit the size of hazel nuts. Also known as Monkey-nut palm.
Immortelle tree	A flowering tree, generally planted on mountain slopes to give shade to the coffee plants.

Tropical bird with a distinctive call 'Qu'est-ce-qu'il dit?'; this is interpreted as 'kiskadee'. Lives in gardens, open woodlands and at the edge of forests.

Kiskadee

A type of large American oppossum, a nocturnal animal, grey-black or reddish in colour, with head markings; lives in rocky crevices or piles of leaves.

Manicou

A type of syrup made from cane juice.

Molasses

One of the largest and strongest of tropical trees. Makes excellent shade for coffee and cocoa bushes; bears beautiful blossoms.

Poui tree

A form of broken French spoken in rural areas of the islands.

Patois

Sapodilla

A brown fruit about the size of a peach which has sweet, soft flesh and hard black seeds.

Sugar cake

Made from coconut and sugar; similar to coconut ice.

'Rain rain go to Spain, And never come back to Trinidad again' is a rhyme which children chant to this day to ward off rain.